THE CASE OF THE DISAPPEARING
BONES

SUE CASON

illustrated by **ROBERT DICKINS**

For information regarding permission, write to:
Sundance Publishing
P.O. Box 740
One Beeman Road
Northborough, MA 01532

Published by:
Sundance Publishing
P.O. Box 740
One Beeman Road
Northborough, MA 01532

Copyright © text Sue Cason
Copyright © illustrations Robert Dickins
Project commissioned and managed by
Lorraine Bambrough-Kelly, The Writer's Style
Cover and text design by Marta White

First published 1996 by
Addison Wesley Longman Australia Pty Limited
95 Coventry Street
South Melbourne 3205 Australia
Exclusive United States Distribution: Sundance Publishing

ISBN 0-7608-0764-7

CONTENTS

Chapter 1

The Scene of the Crime   5

Chapter 2

Lulu   13

Chapter 3

On the Scent   27

Chapter 4

The Chase   43

Chapter 5

The Dogged Detectives   55

Tailpiece   64

CHAPTER 1
THE SCENE
OF THE
CRIME

The small brown dog peered into the hole
in the garden.

"I don't believe it," he muttered.
"I have been robbed. Me!
Detective Dominic Dachshund!"
He threw back his head and howled.

There was a scuffling from behind the fence.
The head and two paws of Detective Max
Dalmatian appeared over the top.

"I was having a quiet scratch," he barked,
"but did I hear you correctly, Dominic?
Did you say you have been robbed?"

"It's true," sniffed Dominic, his ears drooping. "I came to dig up last Monday's bone, and it was gone. Vanished! Disappeared!"

"Maybe you were digging in the wrong place," suggested Max.

Dominic snuffled. "Don't be silly. Detectives don't forget where they bury their bones. It's my job to remember things. Remember?"

"Perhaps you could dig up another bone," said Max.

"And there's another problem," said Dominic sadly. "Look!"

Max leaned over the fence.

In Dominic's backyard were sixteen small piles of soil next to sixteen small holes.

Freshly dug holes.

Empty holes.

"Well," said Max, "it looks like a job for the Dog Squad. I'll come over and see if the thief left any clues."

He leaped over the fence in one bound. "Now are you sure you left the missing bone here?"

"I *know* I left it here," said Dominic firmly, "twenty inches underground."

They both peered into the empty hole.
Max looked at Dominic. "Well, it's not here now."

"It looks like we have a crime to solve," said Dominic. "And we'll have to start from scratch."

"No, thank you," said Max politely, "I've already had one."
Then he glanced at the ground. "Well, what do you think of this?" he barked excitedly. "A clue!"

CHAPTER 2
LULU

"Clue number one," panted Max, "a piece of blue ribbon."

The ribbon was damp and limp and partly covered with soil.

"I know who wears ribbons like that,"
barked Dominic excitedly, "it's that big, fluffy
cat who lives across the road . . . Lulu!"

"Are you sure?" asked Max, his eyes glistening.

"Positively positive," declared Dominic. "Let's interrogate the suspect." He picked up the ribbon with his teeth.

"No," said Max, bounding toward the front gate, "let's visit that cat and ask some questions."

Together they trotted across the road.

Lulu was sprawled on the mailbox, fast asleep.

"Madam," barked Max,
"this is Detective Dominic Dachshund
and I am Detective Max Dalmatian.
Would you answer a few questions about a
robbery?"

8 LETTERS
Kneebone Street.

Lulu opened one green eye.

"A robbery?" she meowed.

Max nodded. "A robbery. We found this ribbon at the scene of the crime," he said. "Is it yours?"

"Mine?" Lulu yowled. "Mine? A *blue* ribbon? No! I wear only *pink*." She glanced at Dominic. "But," she added, "doesn't your owner wear ribbons in her hair? It could belong to her."

"Hmm," Max muttered to himself, "this clever cat could be setting a false trail." He leaned close to Lulu, watching her very carefully. "So, Lulu," he said, "have you *ever* been in the backyard of Number Seven Kneebone Street?"

"Mmmmmmaybe," she said, flicking her long white tail. "Maybe I've passed through there, in the moonlight, on the way to the Cats' Choir for a chorus or two of a well-known song at midnight."

"Aha!" said Dominic, "but have you been there today?"

"Of course not," said Lulu sleepily. "I'm a night person. I rest in the day." She yawned and stretched her paws.

"Someone stole my bones," said Dominic,
"and we're going to find out who did it."

"Well, it wouldn't be me," sniffed Lulu.
"Why would I want *dog* bones? Mewww!
The very thought of it makes my fur stand on end."

8 LETTERS
Kneebone Street

Max glanced at Lulu's long white fur.

"Mmmph," he grunted, "come on,
Detective Dominic, I've got an idea."

"What is it? What is it?" barked Dominic.
"What have you thought of ?"

As they bounded back across the road,
Max leaned down and whispered to his friend,
"Lulu doesn't know anything. I'm sure she's
innocent. But I want to check the ground again
in your backyard. There are sure to be footprints
in that soft soil."

CHAPTER 3
ON THE SCENT

They rushed to the holes and inspected the soil.
It was soft and covered in shoeprints and
two kinds of pawprints.

Dominic sniffed the ground. His nose wrinkled.
"I know that smell," he said.

Max put his black nose to the ground, too.
He snuffled the soil. "And I know *that* smell,"
he declared. "It's us! And those are the
footprints of your owner and her friend.
But *they* wouldn't want your bones."

"Well," said Dominic, "a lot of good that does. We're no further ahead in our investigations."

"Oh, yes we are," said Max. "I think our thief is someone without pawprints."

"Pardon?" said Dominic. "Did you say, *without* pawprints?"

"Precisely," said Max.

"Our thief is pawless."

"So that means," began Dominic,
his eyes gleaming, "that our next suspect is ..."

"Someone who likes bones and has no paws,"
finished Max.

"Ants?" said Dominic, staring at a long line of
ants disappearing into an ant nest.
"Ants have stolen all of my bones?"

"No," said Max. "Follow me,
and we'll question our next suspect."

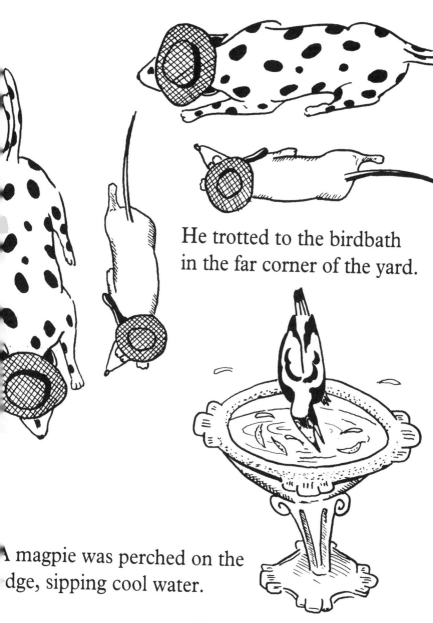

He trotted to the birdbath
in the far corner of the yard.

A magpie was perched on the
dge, sipping cool water.

"Aha," said Max, "I bet she's washing away the evidence. Excuse me, Miss Magpie, could we ask you a few questions regarding a theft in the neighborhood?"

"I didn't do it," twittered the magpie.
"Nobody saw me do it. You can't prove a thing."

'Terrible borrowers, magpies," muttered Max.
'No one is accusing you of anything,
Miss Magpie," he said soothingly, "but we *would*
ike you to help us with our investigations."

"All right," she said grumpily, shaking her feathers, "but whatever it is, I didn't do it."

"Were you in *this* yard this morning after breakfast and before bone time?" asked Dominic.

"Of course I was," answered Miss Magpie, "I was grabbing grubs from the grass."

"And were you involved in any *digging* today?"
he asked.

"Of course I was involved in digging. How do
you think I get the grubs? They don't just lie
around waiting to be swallowed, you know!"
She wiped her beak on the side of the birdbath.

"And did you find anything large and white and smelling delicious while you were digging?" Dominic persisted.

Miss Magpie put her head on one side and thought for a moment. "As a matter of fact, I did," she said slowly.

"And what was it?" panted
Dominic, edging closer to her.

"The biggest, fattest, whitest grub I have ever
seen," said Miss Magpie. "It was absolutely
delicious." She shook her feathers.

Max growled softly as he stepped foward.
"Let me come straight to the point, Miss Magpie.
Did you, or did you not, remove from this yard
sixteen bones belonging to Dominic Dachshund?"

"Bones?" squawked Miss Magpie. "Bones! Why would *I* want bones?" She spread her wings and flew off to a tall tree, chuckling at the very idea.

"Hmm," said Max, "perhaps we've been barking up the wrong tree. Let's return to the scene of the crime."

CHAPTER 4

THE CHASE

"So what have we got?" said Max. "A blue ribbon. No pawprints except our own . . . "
"And sixteen empty bone holes," said Dominic sadly. "That's not much to go on, Max."
"Wait," yelped Max. "Look what's passing the gate right now."

Dominic stared.

The beagle who lived at Number Five trotted past.
In his mouth, he carried a large juicy bone.

"Stop!" Dominic called.

"Stop in the name of the law!"

He bounded to the footpath.

The beagle looked at the small, fierce dog.
Then he gripped the bone more tightly
between his teeth and ran for his life.

Max and Dominic chased him.

They chased the beagle twice around the oak tree and almost caught up to him, but he dashed into his yard and slammed the gate shut.

He dropped the bone and, panting loudly, looked at them from behind the wooden pickets.

"I asked you to stop in the name of the law,"
puffed Dominic, whose small legs allowed
him to run only short distances.

"Why?" asked the beagle suspiciously.

"Dog Squad," said Max. "We want to ask you a few questions."

"Oh," said the beagle, "is that all? I thought you wanted my bone."

"Well . . . " began Dominic, looking hopeful.

"Just a few questions, sir," continued Max. "Where *did* you get that bone?"

"I work the dogwatch in the car lot," explained the beagle. "I keep watch for burglars and thieves. And this is my pay."
He sniffed the bone loudly.

"Oh," said Dominic in a small voice.
"I've had a burglary at my house.
All of my bones are missing, right back
to Friday's bone, two weeks ago."

"Really?" said the beagle. "Why didn't you say
so? I might be able to help you."

"Have you any information that might lead
to solving this crime?" said Max.

"Maybe," said the beagle. "As I came past the
park, I saw two suspicious characters. One of
them had a sack. Inside the sack was something
that smelled delicious. And I heard it rattle. The
other suspicious character carried a large book.
I think it was a book about prehistoric animals."

"Aha!" woofed Max.

"I hope this is a *good* clue, Chief," said Dominic, "because all of this chasing clues makes me dog-tired."

"It *is* a very good clue, Detective Dom," said Max. "I think we're about to collar the suspects."

54

CHAPTER 5

THE DOGGED DETECTIVES

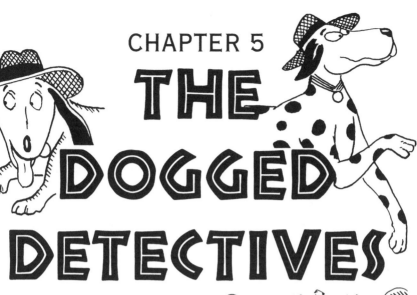

Max and Dominic hid behind a bush in the park.
They peeped through the leaves.

Two figures sat under a tree. They were very
busy making something.

"The criminals?" whispered Dominic.

"Has to be!" said Max.

"I can see soil on the soles of their shoes," said Dominic.

"Dirty thieves!" muttered Max.

"And one of them is wearing only one blue ribbon," Dominic yelped excitedly.

"Evidence!" said Max.

"Shall we charge them?" asked Dominic.

"Definitely!" said Max.

"All right, then," gasped Dominic.

"CHARGE!"

The two detectives leaped from the bush. They ran, barking loudly at the two bone burglars, who were so surprised that they dropped the bones they were holding.

Detective Max, being the bigger dog, grabbed the sack in his teeth and ran off.

Detective Dominic grabbed the bone that was on the grass and rushed down the road after his friend.

here was a wail from one of the robbers.
he one with only one blue ribbon.

Oh no!" she shouted. "You stupid dogs!"

Yikes!" said the other robber, the one holding
he book open to the picture of a dinosaur
keleton. "*Now* how will we make a model of a
rachiosaur for our school project?"

TAILPIECE

Detective Max Dalmatian helped his
friend Detective Dominic Dachshund
gather all of the missing bones.

They didn't make a model of
dinosaur. But they did make
great feast.